TO MY UNCLE AND MY FAVOURITE
LITTLE ARTISTS SÓLEY, ABRIL, JOAN,
CARLES AND MILA. ☺

First published 2013 by Macmillan Children's Books
an imprint of Pan Macmillan
This edition published 2020 by Macmillan Children's Books
The Smithson, 6 Briset Street, London EC1M 5NR
EU representative: Macmillan Publishers Ireland Ltd, 1st Floor,
The Liffey Trust Centre, 117-126 Sheriff Street Upper,
Dublin 1, D01 YC43
www.panmacmillan.com

(PB) ISBN: 978-1-5290-4507-9
(EB) ISBN: 978-1-4472-6994-6

Text and illustrations copyright © Marta Altés 2013
Moral rights asserted.

3 5 7 9 8 6 4

A CIP catalogue record for this book is available
from the British Library.

Printed in China

I AM AN ARTIST

MARTA ALTÉS

MACMILLAN CHILDREN'S BOOKS

I am an artist.

So is my mum!

But in a VERY different way.

Everywhere I look, I see ART.

But I don't think my mum always sees it.

Where I see *The Loneliness of the Carrot,*

my mum sees *An Unfinished Dinner.*

Where I see *A Window to the World,*

my mum sees *A Hole in the Wall.*

(I don't think she understands me.)

But I CAN'T STOP CREATING!

Some of my finest pieces of art this week are:

Blue Number 10,

Blue Number 11,

and *Blue Number 12.*

This one is my *Multiple Self Portrait.*

And I think I'll call this one,
Spring in Winter.

I am SO talented,
I just can't help it.

EVERYTHING

inspires me!

I love NATURE

MOVEMENT

TEXTURES

and SHAPES

But there's just one problem . . .

my mum.

I think maybe something is wrong.
Perhaps I haven't given her enough attention.

There must be something I can do
to make her feel better . . .

mmmmmmmmm . . .

I KNOW!!

I am going to make an AMAZING
piece of art, especially for her.

But it will need plenty of careful planning.

I can't wait for her to wake up.

I hope she likes it!

I call it,
Ode to My Mum.